FLUTE *Debut*

12
EASY PIECES
FOR BEGINNERS

JAMES RAE

James Rae: Flute Debut

Illustrations by Wendy Sinclair
Cover design by Lynette Williamson
CD recorded, mixed and mastered by Simon Painter
with Ian Clarke, flute

UE 21 528
ISMN 979-0-008-08304-4
UPC 8-03452-06677-4
ISBN 978-3-7024-6964-1

Contents / Inhalt / Table des matières

Preface

This collection of twelve very easy original pieces was written with the aim of providing players in the earliest stage of their musical development with solo and group performance material. Although very elementary, the pieces are composed in a wide variety of styles in order to provide a well-balanced musical diet for the young performer.

The pieces fall into three categories:

A — Solos with accompaniment (pieces 1–4)

B — Ensembles with accompaniment (pieces 5 – 8)

C — Ensembles with accompaniment which can be used with books for other instruments in the Debut series (pieces 9 –12)

All the pieces in the book can be performed as solos with piano accompaniment. Chord symbols have been added where appropriate.

Free Downloads:
• piano accompaniments
• illustrations for colouring

⟶ www.universaledition.com/flutedebut

Vorwort

Diese Sammlung von zwölf sehr leichten Kompositionen wurde mit der Absicht geschrieben, SpielerInnen am Anfang ihrer Karriere die Möglichkeit zu geben, sowohl alleine als auch in der Gruppe musizieren zu können. Obwohl alle Stücke technisch einfach sind, flossen viele musikalische Stile ein, um ein möglichst ausgewogenes Bild unserer Hörgewohnheiten zu präsentieren.
Die Stücke sind in drei Kategorien einteilbar:

A   Soli mit Begleitung (Nr. 1– 4)

B   Ensembles mit Begleitung (Nr. 5 – 8)

C   Ensembles mit Begleitung, die mit Heften für andere Instrumente aus der Debut-Reihe kombiniert werden können (Nr. 9 –12)

Alle Stücke aus diesem Heft können als Soli mit Klavierbegleitung aufgeführt werden. Akkordangaben wurden je nach Bedarf hinzugefügt.

Gratis Downloads:
* Klavierbegleitungen
* Illustrationen zum Ausmalen

⟶   www.universaledition.com/flutedebut

Préface

Ce recueil de douze pièces originales très faciles a été conçu pour offrir aux flûtistes en tout début de formation l'occasion de jouer seuls ou à plusieurs. Afin d'assurer aux jeunes musiciens un régime musical équilibré, les pièces, bien que très élémentaires, sont écrites dans une grande diversité de styles.

Le recueil comprend trois types de morceaux :

A   Solos avec accompagnement (pièces 1 à 4)

B   Ensembles avec accompagnement (pièces 5 à 8)

C   Ensembles avec accompagnement compatibles avec les recueils de la série « Débuts » pour d'autres instruments (pièces 9 à 12).

Toutes les pièces peuvent être interprétées par une seule flûte avec accompagnement de piano. Des symboles d'accords ont été ajoutés lorsque nécessaire.

Téléchargements gratuits :
*   accompagnements au piano
*   illustrations à colorier

→   www.universaledition.com/flutedebut

James Rae

Flute Debut

CD 2 / 3

High Street Trot

Beim Einkaufsbummel / Au trot sur la grand-rue

James Rae
(*1957)

*) *Geschäftig* / Affairé

Universal Edition UE 21528

Diva Waltz

Diva-Walzer / La valse de la diva

James Rae

*) *Anmutiges Walzertempo* / Gracieux, tempo de valse

CD 4 / 5

UE 21528

CD 6/7

Sahara Sunset

Sonnenuntergang in der Sahara / Coucher de soleil sur le Sahara

James Rae

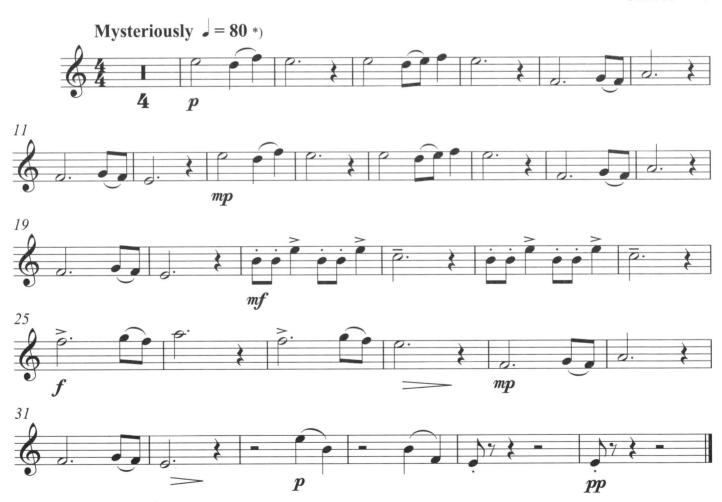

*) *Geheimnisvoll* / Mystérieusement

UE 21528

Funky Street

CD 8/9

James Rae

*) *Beständiges Funktempo* / Tempo funk bien affirmé

UE 21 528

6

Texas Boogie

CD 10/11

James Rae

Steadily rolling along ♩ = 120 (♫ = ♪³♪) *)

*) *Stetig vorwärts gehen* / En avançant toujours

UE 21 528

Texas Boogie

James Rae

UE 21528

The Station Clock

Die Bahnhofsuhr / L'horloge de la gare

CD 12/13

James Rae

Gently ticking ♩ = 120 *)

*) *Sanft tickend* / Avec un doux tic-tac

UE 21528

The Station Clock

Die Bahnhofsuhr / L'horloge de la gare

James Rae

*) *Sanft tickend* / Avec un doux tic-tac

UE 21 528

CD 14/15

The Ogre from the Big Black Rock

Das Ungeheuer vom großen schwarzen Felsen / L'ogre du Gros rocher noir

James Rae

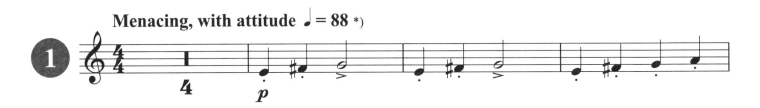

*) *Bedrohlich, mit Haltung* / Menaçant, avec superbe

UE 21 528

The Ogre from the Big Black Rock

Das Ungeheuer vom großen schwarzen Felsen / L'ogre du Gros rocher noir

James Rae

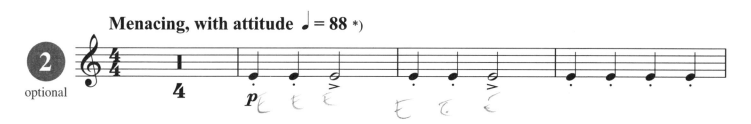

*) *Bedrohlich, mit Haltung* / Menaçant, avec superbe

© Copyright 2011 by Universal Edition A.G., Wien

UE 21 528

Lullaby for a Llama

Schlaflied für ein Lama / Berceuse pour un lama

CD 16/17

James Rae

UE 21528

Lullaby for a Llama

Schlaflied für ein Lama / Berceuse pour un lama

James Rae

UE 21528

Big Chief Sitting Bull

Großer Häuptling Sitting Bull / Le grand Sitting Bull

James Rae

Strongly, with heap big beat!

*) *Kräftig, mit vielen schweren Beats!* / Affirmé, en appuyant bien les temps

CD 18/19

UE 21528

Big Chief Sitting Bull

Großer Häuptling Sitting Bull / Le grand Sitting Bull

James Rae

*) *Kräftig, mit vielen schweren Beats!* / Affirmé, en appuyant bien les temps

UE 21528

I Say, I Say, I Say!

Hört, hört, hört! / J'en ai une bonne

CD 20/21

James Rae

In a bright 'show 2' *)

round and round ad lib.

(on CD: 3x)

*) *In einem schnellen, lebhaften Zweier-Takt. Beliebig oft wiederholen (auf der CD: 3x).*
Vif, à la blanche. Répéter ad libitum (sur le CD : 3 fois).

UE 21528

I Say, I Say, I Say!

Hört, hört, hört! / J'en ai une bonne

James Rae

*) In einem schnellen, lebhaften Zweier-Takt. Beliebig oft wiederholen (auf der CD: 3x).
Vif, à la blanche. Répéter ad libitum (sur le CD : 3 fois).

UE 21528

Dance of the Seven Dachshunds

Tanz der sieben Dackel / La danse des sept teckels

James Rae

*) *In einem flotten „Gassi"-Schritt* / Animé (pensez à un petit chien qui gambade !)

CD 22/23

UE 21528

Dance of the Seven Dachshunds

Tanz der sieben Dackel / La danse des sept teckels

James Rae

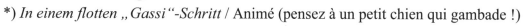

*) *In einem flotten „Gassi"-Schritt* / Animé (pensez à un petit chien qui gambade !)

UE 21528

Marvo the Wondrous Magician

Marvo, der wundersame Magier / Marvo, le fabuleux magicien

James Rae

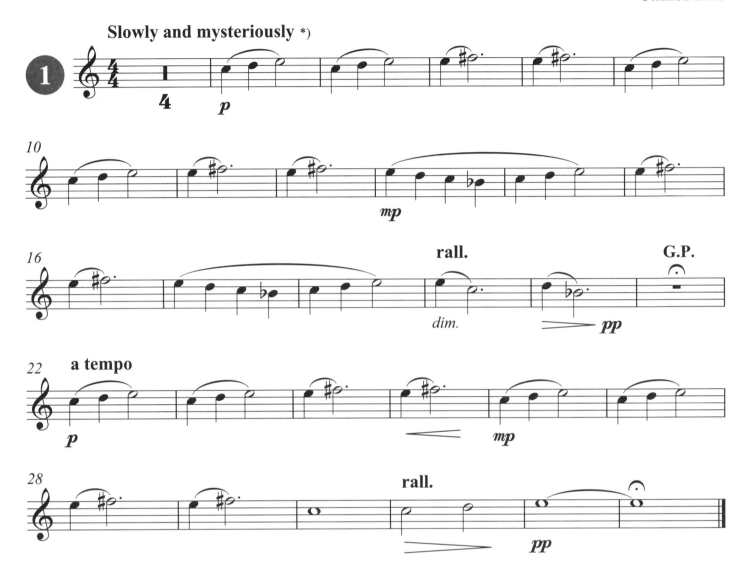

*) *Langsam und geheimnisvoll* / Lent et mystérieu

CD 24 / 25

UE 21 528

Marvo the Wondrous Magician

Marvo, der wundersame Magier / Marvo, le fabuleux magicien

James Rae

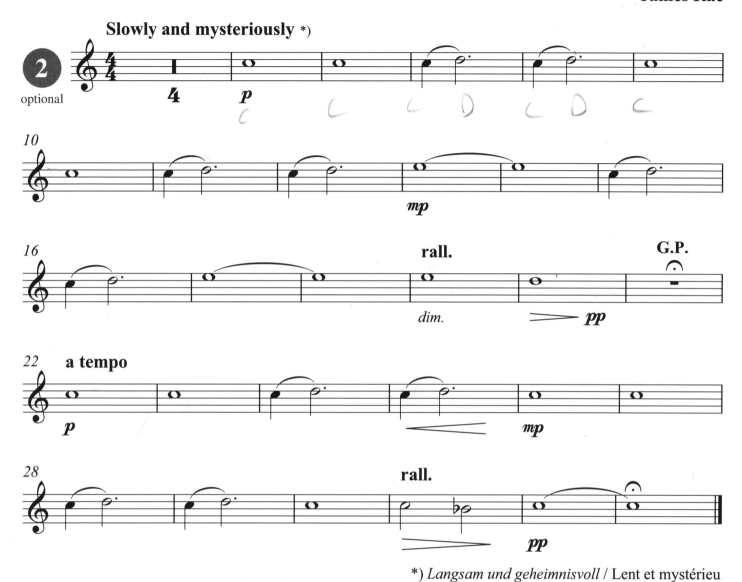

*) *Langsam und geheimnisvoll* / Lent et mystérieu

UE 21528

James Rae • Play it Cool – Flute

Ten easy pieces for clarinet and piano or CD • UE 21 101

Ten solo performance pieces for the beginner in a variety of styles including Swing, Funk, Reggae, Blues and Latin.

The accompaniments, either piano or the CD of orchestrated backings, are strong and supportive taking the player straight into the right stylistic environment.

The CD also features demonstration solos

Ideal for group tuition.

These pieces are available for other instruments making Play it Cool suitable as elementary ensemble material.

Zehn Konzertstücke für Anfänger in verschiedenen Musikstilen wie Swing, Funk, Reggae, Blues und Latin.

Die Klavierbegleitungen und die Play-Along-Versionen auf der beiliegenden CD unterstützen den Spieler, indem sie ihm u.a. sofort einen Eindruck des richtigen Stils vermitteln.

Die CD enthält auch Hörbeispiele der Solos.

Besonders für den Gruppenunterricht geeignet.

Da diese Stücke auch in Ausgaben für andere Instrumente vorliegen, eignet sich Play it Cool hervorragend für junge Ensembles.